Seekers IN Sneakers

A Creative Devotional For Young People

SHARRON OYER, KELLY CANNON, JEAN TORJUSSEN

HARVEST HOUSE PUBLISHERS
Eugene, Oregon 97402

Scripture quotations in this book are taken from
the Holy Bible, New International Version,
Copyright © 1978 by the New York International
Bible Society. Used by permission of
Zondervan Bible Publishers.

SEEKERS IN SNEAKERS

Copyright © 1988 by Harvest House Publishers
Eugene, Oregon 97402

ISBN 0-89081-611-5

Printed in the United States of America.

Sneak Preview

Who? Elementary-age children will enjoy the daily adventures and activities with Templeton and his dog, Furlock.

What? Remind your child to have a Bible, a pencil, and *Seekers in Sneakers* before beginning.

When & Where? Choose the same quiet place and time to help your child develop a consistent Christian walk.

Why? Help your child acquire a love and understanding of God and His Word through the use of this daily devotional. Encourage your child to memorize scripture through the use of the perforated page at the front of the book.

What's Covered?

S earching God's Treasure Book (The Bible)

E xploring God's Handiwork (God's Creation)

E ntering God's Kingdom (Salvation and Assurance)

K eeping in Step (First Steps of Christian Growth)

E xercising Right Attitudes (Becoming Like Jesus)

R ealizing God's Majesty (The Attributes of God)

S pringing into Action (The Daily Walk with God)

Contents

WEEK THREE: Salvation and Assurance

MAN ALIVE
  Creation of Man

THE APPLE OF ADAM'S EYE
  Creation of Woman

GOD'S GREEN ACRE
  Life in the Garden of Eden

THE BIGGEST BLOOPER
  The Fall of Adam and Eve

BETTER THAN DISNEYLAND
  Heaven

GOD'S MAP TO HEAVEN
  Salvation

SURE ENOUGH
  Assurance

WEEK FOUR: First Steps of Growth

HAPPY BIRTHDAY TO YOU
  New Life

FAMILY PHOTOS
  God's Family

MEET YOUR "STAY-WITHIN FRIEND"
  Eternal Security

HOTLINE TO HEAVEN
  Prayer

THE CONTEST
  Prayer Power

PARDON ME
  Confession

GIVE IT ALL TO GOD
  Consecration

God's Way to Heaven

If you would like to receive the Lord Jesus as your Savior, you can do it now by:

A—Admitting to God you've done wrong things.

"For all have sinned . . ." (Romans 3:23).

B—Believing that the Lord Jesus, God's Son, died for you on the cross, giving His life's blood to take your punishment, and is the only one who can take away your sins (the wrong things you've done).

". . . Christ died for our sins . . . He was buried . . . He was raised on the third day . . ." (1 Corinthians 15:3,4).

C—Claiming His promise of everlasting life.

". . . whoever believes in Him shall not perish [be separated from God forever] but have eternal life" (John 3:16).

You can say something like this to God:

"Dear God, I know I have done wrong things. I believe You died for me and You are the only one who can take away my sins. Right now I claim Your promise of everlasting life—the kind of life I need to live in heaven with You someday and to be a winner here on earth. Thank You. In Jesus' name, Amen.

Dear Parents,

How do you enrich your child's understanding of God's Word? How do you motivate your child to spend time in the Bible? How do you relate Biblical principles to the problems your child is facing in today's society?

Do these questions concern you? *Seekers in Sneakers* can be a valuable tool in accomplishing the goal of meeting the spiritual needs of your child.

To use this devotional effectively, help your child choose a quiet place where he can go at the same time every day. An NIV Bible (New International Version) and a pencil will be necessary to complete the lessons. A special verse is suggested on the top of the first lesson of each week to encourage your child to memorize God's Word. A perforated page with these key verses is provided at the back of the book.

Our prayer is that the daily adventures of Templeton and Furlock will open your child's eyes to the wonders of God and His universe. The time your child spends with God in His Word will benefit him today and for eternity.

In Christ,

Jean, Kelly, Sharron

Jean, Kelly, and Sharron

Weekly Verse: Isaiah 44:6b

Who Is It?

Furlock **Templeton**

Have you ever dreamed of being someone famous? Like a famous movie star, singer, baseball player, or someone else?

Who do you think is the most famous person in the world? Here are three clues. Can you help Templeton and Furlock figure out who it is?

CLUE 1
He sees through walls, ceilings, and doors;
Even the plants on the ocean floors!
He can see anything in the darkest night,
To Him, the darkness is as light.

CLUE 2
He knows each person on earth by name
And He alone remains the same.
He knows everything **you** say and do,
Your secret thoughts, He knows them, too.

CLUE 3
He never is in just one place,
He's everywhere — on earth, in space.
Wherever **you** go, whatever **you** do,
He's always there watching **you**!

Isaiah 46:9
I am God, and there is no other; . . . there is none like Me.

Who is this famous person?
God, of course! (Did you guess right?)
He is the most famous person in the world because He can do *anything*!

GO

DISCOVER WHAT GOD IS LIKE

Find and circle every word in the letter maze below which describes what God is like. The words you are looking for are listed below. They may be found in the maze written up, down, across, or diagonally. Each time you find one, color in the magnifying glass that matches.

```
A M L F L U F R E W O P G
C X U A W X T S G R E A T
P T F I O I L A N R E T E
L R I T F Y S X F H X I U
U N C H A N G E A B L E K
S P R F I Z C O J Z N N M
T N E U R T G B O X H T S
H X M L O V I N G D D X F
```

SOME WONDERFUL THINGS ABOUT GOD. GOD IS

- **GOOD:** God is full of kindness.
- **GREAT:** God is mighty and wonderful
- **FAIR:** God always makes the right decisions.
- **POWERFUL:** God can do anything He wants to.
- **PERFECT:** God is completely pure. He hates sin.
- **WISE:** God knows how to do everything.
- **TRUE:** God never lies. He keeps His promises.
- **UNCHANGEABLE:** God has never changed and never will.
- **PATIENT:** God has complete control over Himself.
- **FAITHFUL:** God always does what He says He will do.
- **MERCIFUL:** God can forgive us when we don't deserve it.
- **LOVING:** God desires the best for you.
- **ETERNAL:** God has no beginning and no ending.

God's Perfect Son

(John 1:14)

Can you help Templeton figure out the right answer?

Yes, JESUS is the right answer! He was God the Son and Perfect Man all in one person. He lived in heaven before coming to earth, and even at your age He *never* did anything wrong—*ever*! He never talked back to His mother, Mary, or earthly father, Joseph. Jesus never got scared. He always knew all the right answers, and He was *always* kind to His brothers and sisters.

That's why Jesus could take the punishment for your sin. And to prove He was "God in a body," He came back to life after He died, and He is living in heaven today!

The Word [God the Son] became flesh [put on skin and bones] and lived for a while among us . . . [here on earth].
John 1:14

JESUS IS: GOD THE SON
JESUS BECAME: PERFECT MAN

Read each sentence. If the statement is true, circle the letter under the "T." If the sentence is false, circle the letter under the "F."

		T	F
1.	Jesus came back to life after He died.	J	L
2.	Many other people have come back to life by their own power.	A	E
3.	Mohammed and Buddha are alive today in heaven.	T	S
4.	Jesus is the only perfect person who ever lived.	U	M
5.	You can become perfect if you try real hard.	H	S
6.	Jesus lived in heaven before coming to earth as a baby.	I	O
7.	Buddha and Mohammed were perfect.	R	S
8.	Jesus is the only person who could die for your sin.	A	B
9.	Believing in Jesus is the only way to heaven.	L	C
10.	Jesus is living in California.	X	I
11.	Jesus cares about **you.**	V	D
12.	You can be good enough to get to heaven.	A	E

To discover the secret message, fill in the blanks with the letters you circled.

__ __ __ __   __ __   __ __ __ __ __

Since Jesus is alive, He can give you everlasting life. Everlasting life is the kind of life you need to live in heaven. When you believe in Him and receive His gift of everlasting life, He can help you with the hard times at home with your parents, with brothers and sisters, with schoolwork, and with scary things that happen.

In the space below, list some things that are giving you a hard time. Then, thank Jesus for being alive to help you!

Remember, Jesus cares about **you!**

11

Always the Same: God Is Unchanging—Part 1

(Malachi 3:6) 1 Thessalonians 5:18

Templeton is taking a survey. Check how you would answer the statements below about yourself. Be honest, please!

SURVEY _____ Templeton

	ALWAYS	OFTEN	SOMETIMES	SELDOM	NEVER
I am kind.					
I do what I'm told.					
I keep my promises.					
Everything I say is right.					
I get along with my brothers and sisters.					
I change my mind.					
I am happy.					

GO

If you were completely honest, I'm sure your chart looks like all the other ones Templeton has collected. There would be check marks in all different places. If Templeton asked you to fill out this same chart next year, some of your answers would probably change, because **you** are changing! You look different as you grow older, and you become smarter as you learn new things.

Did you know that God never changes His mind about anything? The way God thought before He created the world is the way He thinks today. He never gets smarter because He's as smart as anyone could ever get. He knows everything and He is always right.

Have you ever talked someone into doing something they said they wouldn't do? Or maybe your friends have talked you into something you knew you shouldn't do! That can't happen to God. Neither you nor anyone else can talk Him into anything that isn't for your very best.

I the Lord do not change.
Malachi 3:6

A circle can remind you that God has no beginning and no end, and that He always is the same.

Templeton has discovered words for two things about God that never change. Can you find the words in the circles and write them in the spaces below the circles? Look up the verses to see if you're right.

1. __ __ __ __
(Psalm 119:89)

2. __ __ __ __
(Jeremiah 31:3)

1. God's _____ will not change. He always does what He has promised to do. You can count on it!

2. God's _____ is everlasting. He loves you as much today as He did yesterday, and He will love you tomorrow as much as He did today. You can count on that, too!

Now take a few minutes to memorize this verse. When you can say it without looking, repeat it to someone in your house who will be glad to know it, too. Ready ... Set ... Memorize!

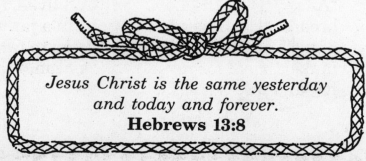

Jesus Christ is the same yesterday and today and forever.
Hebrews 13:8

You Can Depend on It! God Is Unchanging—Part 2

(Numbers 23:19)

"**Y**ou're so wishy-washy!" Have you ever heard that said about people? It means they can't make up their minds or they keep changing their minds about something. Have **you** ever been wishy-washy? Probably everyone has at one time or another. Is God ever wishy-washy? No! He **never** changes what He is like or how He thinks about things. He is ALWAYS THE SAME!

There's a story in the Bible that shows this special quality that belongs only to God.

Find 1 Kings 17 in your Bible. After you read the story in the Bible, put the name of the person who is speaking on the line in front of the words they speak. The characters of the story are: The Lord (God), Elijah, and the widow. Begin in verse 8.

_____ : "Go at once to Zarephath in Sidon and stay there. I have commanded a widow in that place to supply you with food."

Read verse 10. What was the widow doing when Elijah saw her?

_____

_____ : "Would you bring me a little water in a jar so I may have a drink? And bring me, please, a piece of bread."

_____ : "As surely as the Lord your God lives, I don't have any bread—only a handful of flour in a jar and a little oil in a jug. I am gathering a few sticks to take home and make a meal for myself and my son, that we may eat it—and die."

GO

_____ : "Don't be afraid. Go home and do as you have said. But first make a small cake of bread for me from what you have and bring it to me."

_____ : "The jar of flour will not be used up and the jug of oil will not run dry until the day the Lord gives rain on the land."

Now read verses 15 and 16. Did God change His mind after a while and not take care of Elijah and the widow and her son? What happened?

_____

_____

_____

God's love for Elijah, the widow, and her son never changed. If you know the Lord Jesus as your Savior, His love for **you** never changes either. That's why you can depend on Him to ALWAYS take care of you.

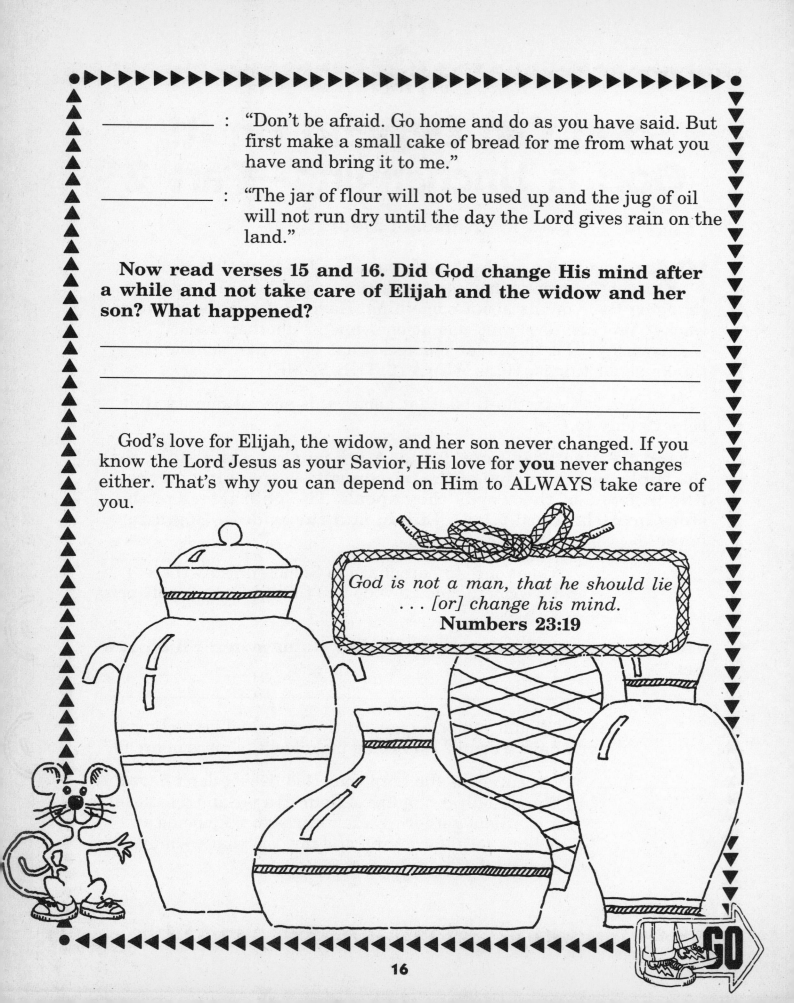

God is not a man, that he should lie . . . [or] change his mind.
Numbers 23:19

GO

Now let's think about some ways that you and I change but God does not. The words on the left are what you and I are like sometimes. The words on the right are exactly the opposite. They tell what God is ALWAYS like. Match the words. The first one is done for you.

What We Are Like

1. UNKIND
2. WRONG
3. BAD
4. IMPATIENT
5. UNFAIR
6. UNFORGIVING
7. UNCARING
8. UNWISE
9. SELFISH
10. WISHY-WASHY

What God Is Like

RIGHT
PATIENT
FAIR
KIND
GOOD
WISE
FORGIVING
UNSELFISH
CARING
THE SAME

Now fill in the sentences below using the words above.

1. Sometimes I am ___Unkind___ but God is always ___Kind___ .

2. Sometimes I am _____ but God is always _____ .

3. Sometimes I am _____ but God is always _____ .

4. Sometimes I am _____ but God is always _____ .

5. Sometimes I am _____ but God is always _____ .

6. Sometimes I am _____ but God is always _____ .

7. Sometimes I am _____ but God is always _____ .

8. Sometimes I am _____ but God is always _____ .

9. Sometimes I am _____ but God is always _____ .

10. Sometimes I am _____ but God is always _____ .

Heaven Sent:
The Bible—God's Word
(2 Timothy 3:16)

"Hi, Templeton! What's wrong with you?"

"My Sunday school teacher said God wrote us a letter, so I'm waiting to get it. I know heaven is a long way off, but it sure is taking a long time!"

"Templeton, God is not going to send you a letter from heaven through the mail!"

"Why not? Would it cost too much postage?"

"No, silly! God has already sent you a letter! I saw it in your house! Come on, I'll show you!"

You probably have a letter from God, too, somewhere in your house, sent "special delivery" from God to **you**! In fact, it's not just one letter, but 66 all wrapped up in one big book. Have you guessed what it's called?

Unscramble the words below to discover the name of this special letter from God:

B = ⊖   H = ⊗   L= ◑   Y= ◐   E= ⊜   I= ◍   O= ●

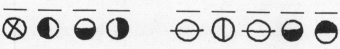

The word "holy" means "wholly good" or 100 percent true. Every single word in the Bible is true because God wrote it! How? Did God type it Himself? Did He write it on a giant scroll and send an angel dressed like a mailman to deliver it? No. God chose 40 men to write down what He said to them. They were like His secretaries as He guided them in knowing what to say and how to say it.

> *All Scripture is God-breathed.*
> **2 Timothy 3:16**

GO

No one knows exactly how God told them what to write. We don't know whether He talked to them out loud or told them quietly in their thoughts. But we can be certain that *all* of the Holy Bible is God's letter to us—*every word*!

Most of the 40 men God used to write the Bible did not know each other at all. They lived at different times in history. In fact, from the time the first man wrote what God told him to write until the last man wrote his part, over 1,600 years had gone by!

Now, let's see how much you remember. Answer the four questions below.

1. What percent of the Bible is true? _____

2. How many men did God use to write the Bible? _____

3. How many years had gone by before the Bible was finished? _____

4. How many "letters" or books are in the Bible? _____

Place each answer in the square that matches the question number.

After you have written your answers in the squares, add the numbers across. Then add your numbers down.

The total of both your answer columns should be 1,806.

Answer 1	Answer 2	
+	=	
Answer 3	Answer 4	
+	=	
		=
+	=	

The Bible is God's special letter to you, so you should read it often and handle it with care!

The best letter to read first is either Mark or John in the New Testament. Find it in your Bible and read a few verses every day. START NOW! Ready . . . Set . . . Read!

STOP

Believe It or Not:
God's Word Is True

(Psalm 119:160)

Fairy tales can be fun to read. They help you imagine faraway places and times. Do you have a favorite fairy tale or make-believe story?

Some people think that God's Word, the Bible, is a book of fairy tales. They think it is full of stories that couldn't have really happened. Some people don't believe the Bible is true. Did a man named Jonah really get swallowed by a giant fish and live in the fish's stomach three whole days (Jonah 1:17)? Did a little shepherd boy really kill a giant with only a slingshot (1 Samuel 17:49,50)? Did Jesus really walk on top of water without sinking (John 6:19)? There are many stories in the Bible that seem make-believe, but God says that every single one really did happen!

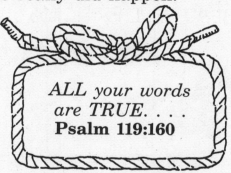

ALL your words are TRUE. . . .
Psalm 119:160

There are many ways to prove the Bible is true. To discover two ways, choose the letters that match the numbers printed in the chart below. The first answer is started for you.

$\frac{1}{A}$	$\frac{2}{B}$	$\frac{3}{C}$	$\frac{4}{D}$	$\frac{5}{E}$	$\frac{6}{F}$	$\frac{7}{G}$	$\frac{8}{H}$	$\frac{9}{I}$	$\frac{10}{J}$	$\frac{11}{K}$	$\frac{12}{L}$	$\frac{13}{M}$
$\frac{14}{N}$	$\frac{15}{O}$	$\frac{16}{P}$	$\frac{17}{Q}$	$\frac{18}{R}$	$\frac{19}{S}$	$\frac{20}{T}$	$\frac{21}{U}$	$\frac{22}{V}$	$\frac{23}{W}$	$\frac{24}{X}$	$\frac{25}{Y}$	$\frac{26}{Z}$

#1. $\frac{P}{16}$ $\frac{R}{18}$ $\frac{}{15}$ $\frac{}{16}$ $\frac{}{8}$ $\frac{}{5}$ $\frac{}{3}$ $\frac{}{25}$

#2. $\frac{}{19}$ $\frac{}{3}$ $\frac{}{9}$ $\frac{}{5}$ $\frac{}{14}$ $\frac{}{3}$ $\frac{}{5}$

PROPHECY

The Bible tells what will happen in the future before it happens. That's what *prophecy* means. Because God knows everything, He told His special writers things that would happen hundreds of years later. Everything has come true just as God said it would!

Look up Micah 5:2 to find out just one of these special promises that came true. Read the verse, then fill in the blank:

God said that when the Lord Jesus came to earth He would be born in the city of

_____ .

This was written *700 years* before it happened! **Now look up Matthew 2:1 to check your answer.**

21

SCIENCE

The Bible told scientific facts before scientists even discovered these facts.

Look up Isaiah 40:22 and fill in the blank:

God sits in heaven above the _____ of the earth. God said the earth was round over *2000 years* before Christopher Columbus discovered it to be a fact!

There are hundreds of ways the Bible proves itself to be the true Word of God. We have talked about just two. Maybe you have a friend who thinks that God's Word is just a book of fairy tales. What could you say to your friend to help him know the truth of what you've learned today?

Write your answer in the Bible below.

Worth More than a Million: The Value of God's Word

(Psalm 119:72)

Templeton and Furlock are excited, and **you** will be, too, when you discover the secret today that they've discovered! You, too, can own the very same thing Templeton has! It only costs a few dollars, but it's worth more than a million! You may already have one! **What is it?** Our verse for today will give you the answer.

$$**      **$$

> *The law from your mouth [God's word, the Bible] is more precious to me than thousands of pieces of silver and gold.*
> **Psalm 119:72**

Many people today are spending lots of money for new things that can never make them happy forever. The new things they buy can't help them when they are lonely, worried, or afraid. Only a special friendship with God can give you the kind of life you need to live in heaven someday with Him and to have a happy life here on earth. God's Word tells you how! It's full of "very great and precious promises."

I'M RICH! I'M RICH! I OWN SOMETHING THAT'S WORTH MORE THAN A MILLION TRILLION ZILLION DOLLARS... ...AND I ONLY HAD TO PAY A FEW BUCKS FOR IT!

GO

Psalm 119 is a special chapter in the Bible that tells many other reasons why God's Word is so valuable.

Find and read each verse. Fill in the crossword puzzle below with the missing words. The first letter of each word is given for you and all the words are found in the Treasure Chest to help you.

ACROSS:

4. Verse 52: I find _____ in God's Word when I'm sad.

6. Verse 104: I gain _____ from God's Word when I'm puzzled or confused.

7. Verse 105: God's Word is a _____ for my path when I don't know what to do.

8. Verse 114: I can put my _____ in God's Word when I'm discouraged.

9. Verse 165: God's Word gives me great _____ when I'm worried or afraid.

10. Verse 98: God's Word makes me _____ than my enemies, those who don't like me.

DOWN:

1. Verse 66: God's Word gives me _____—it teaches me everything I need to know about making God happy

2. Verse 111: God's Word is the _____ of my heart when I'm lonely.

3. Verse 28: God's Word _____ me when I have a hard thing to do.

5. Verse 11: God's Word helps me not to _____—think, say, and do wrong things.

7. Verse 37: God's Word renews my _____—keeps me safe and happy.

9. Verse 9: God's Word keeps my way _____—helps me think, say, and do the right things.

GO

1 K

2 J

3 S

4 C

5 S

6 U

7 L

8 H

9 P

10 W

understanding
sin light joy
wiser

life peace
knowledge pure hope
comfort
strengthens

STOP

25

Weekly Verse: Genesis 1:31a

Custom-Made by God

Creation (Overview) (Genesis 1:1–2:3)

God saw all that he had made, and it was very good.
Genesis 1:31

What's that?

It was supposed to be a birthday cake for my dad

Maybe he can use it for a Frisbee!

Have you ever tried to make something by yourself? Sometimes things just don't turn out like we plan, but God made some things that turned out exactly as He planned.

God made everything you see around you, even people. He made it all in just six days, and on the seventh day He stopped His work and saw that all He made was very good. He just spoke and each thing was created. (Created means made from nothing.) The first things God made were night, day, stars, planets, water, land, plants, and animals. On the sixth day God made man. God made man special because He wanted someone to spend time with and to be friends with. Is the Creator of the world your friend?

GO

Help Templeton unscramble the words that tell some of the things that God made. Draw a picture of each one in the space next to the word. When you're done, turn the book upside down to check your answers.

1. G I N T H

4. S M A N L I A

2. E L P O P E

5. A T S S R

3. S T P A L N

6. A E R W T

Did you unscramble them all?

You Light up My Life

Creation: Day 1 (Genesis 1:2-5)

"Okay, who's the wise guy who turned off all the lights?"

"It sure is dark in here isn't it, Templeton! You're not scared are you?"

"Of course not! Nothin' *ever* scares me!"

"Hey, where did you go?"

"BOO!"

Have you ever been scared in the dark? What do you think it would be like to live in darkness all the time, with no lamps, candles, or flashlights to light up the night? That's how it was in the very beginning, before God made anything. It was so dark that you couldn't see anything at all. But then, there was nothing to see!

On the first day of creation, God decided to change all that!

Use the secret code to find out what God made first and how He did it. Write the correct letter in each blank.

$$\frac{}{1}\ \frac{}{9}\ \frac{}{3}\ \frac{}{5}\ \frac{}{10}\ \frac{}{3}\ \frac{}{12}\ \frac{}{1}\ \frac{}{7}\ \frac{}{3},\ ``\frac{}{8}\ \frac{}{4}\ \frac{}{13}$$

$$\frac{}{13}\ \frac{}{6}\ \frac{}{4}\ \frac{}{11}\ \frac{}{4}\ \frac{}{2}\ \frac{}{4}\ \frac{}{8}\ \frac{}{7}\ \frac{}{5}\ \frac{}{6}\ \frac{}{13},"$$

$$\frac{}{1}\ \frac{}{9}\ \frac{}{3}\ \frac{}{13}\ \frac{}{6}\ \frac{}{4}\ \frac{}{11}\ \frac{}{4}\ \frac{}{14}\ \frac{}{1}\ \frac{}{12}$$

$$\frac{}{8}\ \frac{}{7}\ \frac{}{5}\ \frac{}{6}\ \frac{}{13}."$$ (Genesis 1:3)

SECRET CODE: a = 1; b = 2; d = 3; e = 4; g = 5; h = 6; i = 7; l = 8; n = 8; n = 9; o = 10; r = 11; s = 12; t = 13; w = 14; y = 15

What was the first thing God made? _____

How did He do it? _____

God simply said "light," and light appeared! He made it out of nothing. (Remember, that's what "created" means—to make out of nothing.) After God made light, He saw that it was good. He called the light "__ __ __," and the darkness He called "__ __ __ __ __."

3 1 15   9 7 5 6 13

But remember, no matter if it's day or night, God can see just as well in the darkness as He can in the light! Because He loves you, He wants to take care of you in the daytime *and* the nighttime—*all the time!*

> *Even the darkness will not be dark to you;*
> *the night will shine like the day,*
> *for darkness is as light to you.*
> **Psalm 139:12**

"Hey, I'm sorry, Templeton. That was a pretty mean thing to do!"

"That's okay. How come you're never scared in the dark?"

"'Cause I know God can take care of me no matter how dark it is! He can see just as well in the dark as He can in the light!"

"Wow, I guess that means I can throw away my Mickey Mouse night-light with the fluorescent tennis shoes!"

Answers:
And God said, "Let there be light, and there was light."
day, night

What Am I?

Creation: Day 2 (Genesis 1:6-8)

So God made the expanse and separated the water....
God called the expanse "sky."
Genesis 1:7,8

You cannot see me, I rhyme with chair,

I'm all about you, everywhere.

You cannot taste me, I can't be worn,

but you need me the day you're born.

What am I?

CHAIR − CH = __ __ __

Even though you cannot touch it, air is "something." It's a mixture of oxygen and other invisible gases which God made for you to breathe. Without air you could not live. This is why the astronauts have to wear 30-pound space suits which supply their oxygen, for in outer space there is no air. God has made a circle of air around the earth for you to breathe. Air is part of what God made on the second day of creation. The Bible says,

God made the expanse, or sky,
...the second day.

Air is something we cannot even see, yet it is so very important to us. Can you think of someone who is also invisible now but is important to us? The answer is GOD, of course. You cannot see Him but He is real.

GO

Go around the circle **2** times
skipping every other letter to
help Furlock discover what God made
on the **2**nd day of His creation.

start
here

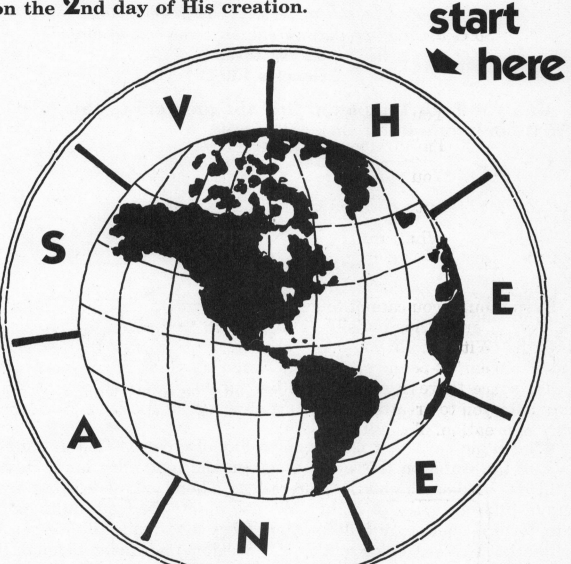

For you to answer:

On the second day of creation God made the

_ _ _ _ _ _ _ _ _

STOP

Tree-mendous

Creation: Day 3 (Genesis 1:9-13)

*God called the dry ground "land," and the gathered
waters he called "seas." ... Then God said,
"Let the land produce vegetation ... according to their
various kinds."*
Genesis 1:10,11

**Can you help Templeton find the answers to this puzzle?
Write only one letter on each blank.**

1. We have these
inside and outside.
Sometimes they are
green.

2. We stand on
this outside.
Farmers grow
plants on it.

3. Sailors cross
these. God parted
one. It rhymes
with sneeze.

Did you solve the puzzle? If you did, you know what God made on
the third day of creation.

The Bible says that on the third day of creation God gathered all
of the water in the world together and made dry land. He called
the dry land earth and the waters seas. Then God made grass, trees,
and different types of plants. We use plants for food, building
materials, shelter, and decoration. They also make the oxygen we
breathe. We see God's great wisdom and caring through His
creation of plants.

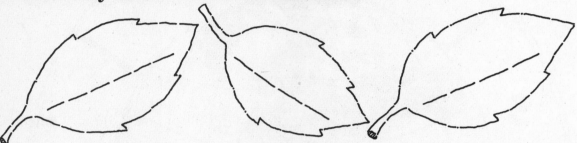

Answers: 1. plants 2. land 3. seas

How many different types of plants are there around your house? How about in your neighborhood?

Can you list some of the different kinds? Write them on the leaves of this plant. After you do, color your plant and think about how wise God is to take care of everything we need.

Out of This World

Creation: Day 4 (Genesis 1:14-19)

God made two great lights—the greater light to govern the day and the lesser light to govern the night. He also made the stars.
Genesis 1:16

Our God who made the "lights" in the sky is so wise. He made the ☀, the 🌙, and the ⭐⭐ each for special reasons. Did you know that life would be impossible without the ☀ today? The atmosphere would freeze. There would be no rain, and all the crops would die. The 🌙 provides the force that causes high and low tides, and just think how dark it would be without the glittery ⭐⭐. God knew just what we would need to live at the very beginning of the world and He also knows what is best for us today.

Next time you are outside on a clear evening, stop to look at the mysterious moon and the twinkling stars and think about how GREAT and WISE our God is. You can even tell Him that you think so right now.

Follow the dots to discover what kind of lights God made for the sky on the 4th day.

35

Templeton needs help finding a verse in the Bible. Look up Isaiah 40:26 and write it below in your best handwriting:

_____

_____

_____

_____

_____

_____

Now help Templeton explain the meaning to Furlock. Write the verse in your own words below.

_____

_____

_____

_____

_____

_____

HEAVEN BOUND

STOP

Feathers and Fins

Creation: Day 5 (Genesis 1:20-23)

So God created the great creatures of the sea . . . and every winged bird. . . . And God saw that it was good.
Genesis 1:21

Close your eyes and think of a world with no people, animals, fish, or birds. The earth must have been a very quiet place the first four days of creation, but all of that changed on the fifth day. God created life in the seas and birds to fly in the air. There are so many different sizes, shapes, and colors that it is hard to imagine. Why are there so many different kinds? Each one has its own purpose. Some birds help carry seeds to spread plant life. Smaller fish are food for larger fish.

Just as God made different kinds of fish and birds for a reason, God made you different for a reason, too. God wants to use the things you do best. Ask God to help you know what to do with your special talent.

WHAT I DO BEST

_____
_____
_____
_____

HOW I CAN USE MY TALENTS FOR GOD

_____
_____
_____
_____

GO

Templeton has written six clues and their answers on his clipboard, but he can't remember which clue goes with which answer. Can you help him? Read the clue, choose the right answer, and fill in the spaces of the puzzle.

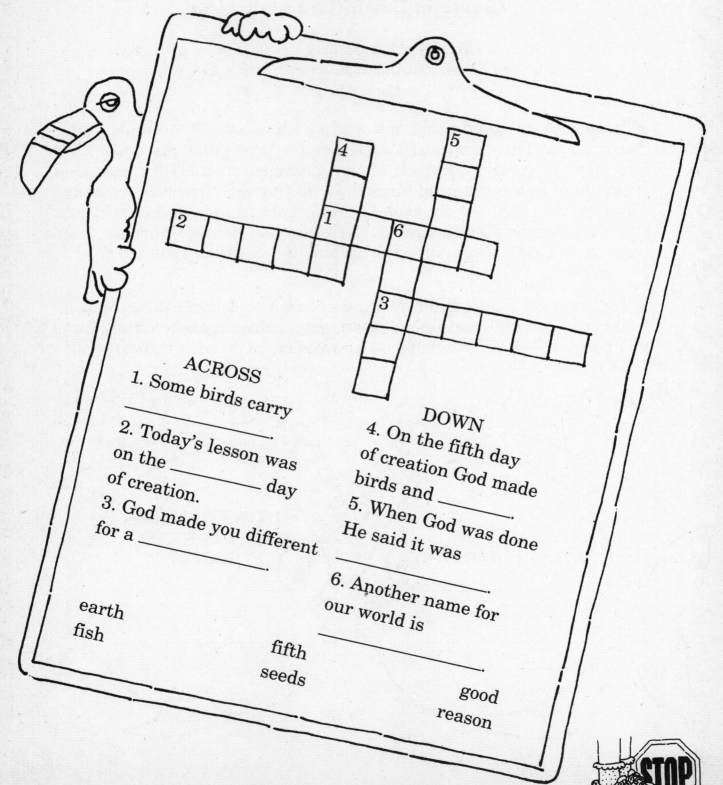

ACROSS
1. Some birds carry
_____.

2. Today's lesson was on the _____ day of creation.

3. God made you different for a _____.

DOWN
4. On the fifth day of creation God made birds and _____.

5. When God was done He said it was _____.

6. Another name for our world is _____.

earth
fish

fifth
seeds

good
reason

Animals, Animals Everywhere!

Creation: Day 6 (Genesis 1:24, 25)

Romans 5:8

Have you ever thought about what an imagination God must have had on the sixth day of creation when He made the animals? Big ones, small ones, short ones, tall ones, spotted, striped, furry, and feathery—just to describe a few! In fact, there are over one million different species, or kinds, of animals that zoologists know about! There are probably many more that we don't know about and never will. God's Word says that God made all the animals "according to their kind" on the same day.

> *God made the wild animals according to their kinds . . . and all the creatures that move along the ground according to their kinds. And God saw that it was good.*
> **Genesis 1:25**

This means that animals did not evolve, or grow into a different kind of animal later on. God created the animals to be the same kind as you see them today! A giraffe will always have a baby giraffe, a cat will always have a baby kitten, and a duck will never lay a turkey egg.

GO

Now, how about a game of Animal Trivia? After reading the clues, unscramble the words to discover which animal the clues describe.

1. I never stop growing as long as I live. I can chew my food underwater but cannot swallow underwater. What am I?

l a t r i a o l g

_____

2. I have 135 rows of teeth with 115 teeth in each row! It's a good thing animals don't have to go to the dentist! What am I?

i n l s a

_____

3. I have four pairs of ears—one of the pairs is on my two front legs! What am I?

n a t

_____

4. I have three eyelids—two to keep out the sand and one to wipe out the dust. What am I?

m l e a c

_____

5. I have approximately 1,000 hollow hairs on the bottom of my six feet. I also have 1,000 facets on my eyes so that although you see just one object, when I look at it I see 1,000! What am I?

y f l

_____

Draw a picture of your pet or favorite kind of animal. Next time you're in the school library, or if you have an encyclopedia at home, find out some unusual information about your animal and write your own trivia clues. Play Animal Trivia with a friend and share God's love!

WEEK 3

DAY ONE

Weekly Verse: Hebrews 13:5b

Man Alive!

Creation of Man (Genesis 1:26-31)

You look just like your father!

Has anyone ever told you that you look or act like someone in your family? You may not be surprised to hear that, but you may be surprised to hear who else you are like—God.

The Bible says that on the sixth day of creation God made man out of the dust of the earth and breathed life into him. Man was made in God's image. God doesn't have hands, fingers, and toes, but we were made to think and have feelings like God.

God wants us to grow to be more like Him by studying His Word, the Bible, and talking to Him. Are you growing more like God every day?

> *The Lord God formed man from the dust of the ground and breathed into his nostrils the breath of life and, man became a living being.* **Genesis 2:7**

GO

Draw a picture of yourself. Do you look like your mother, your father, your aunt, or your cousin?

Now list some ways that you are like God and some ways you can grow to be more like Him. Two ways are listed for you.

WAYS I'M LIKE GOD

I can love.
_____
_____
_____
_____

WAYS I NEED TO GROW TO BE MORE LIKE GOD

Learn to love people who

aren't nice to me.
_____
_____
_____

The Apple of Adam's Eye

Creation of Woman (Genesis 1:26-28; 2:21-23)

Have you ever been lonely? Sometimes it's nice to be alone, but no one likes to be alone all of the time. God cared about the first man, Adam, and did not want him to be lonely. After God made the plants, birds, fish, animals, and man, God saw that Adam needed someone who was made like him to be his friend and helper.

God caused Adam to go into a deep sleep while He took out one of Adam's ribs. Out of Adam's rib God made the first woman, Eve. Eve was to be Adam's friend and helper. They were to live together in the Garden of Eden and spend their lives getting to know God. God wants you to get to know Him better, too. He cares about you just like He cared about Adam. When you're lonely, pray and tell God how you feel. God will always be there.

Then the Lord God made a woman from the rib He had taken out of the man, and He brought her to the man.
Genesis 2:22

44

God has given us many special promises in His Word, the Bible. One of these promises can help when you feel lonely. Look up the verse below and fill in the missing letters to find God's special promise to you.

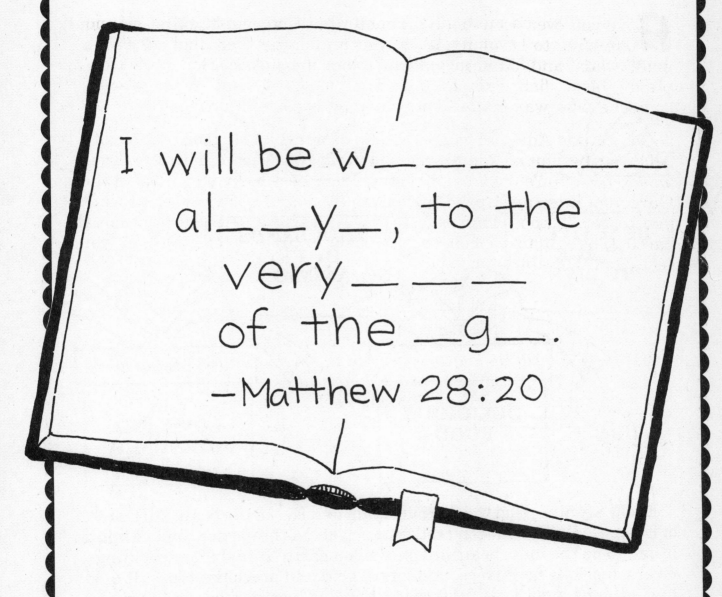

I will be w____ ____ al___y__, to the very____ of the _g__.
—Matthew 28:20

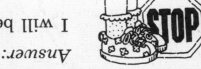

45

God's Green Acres

Life in the Garden of Eden (Genesis 2:8-15)

Gifts, gifts, and more gifts! That's what God gave the first man and woman who ever lived. Do you remember their names? What kinds of gifts did God give them? Here are just a few:

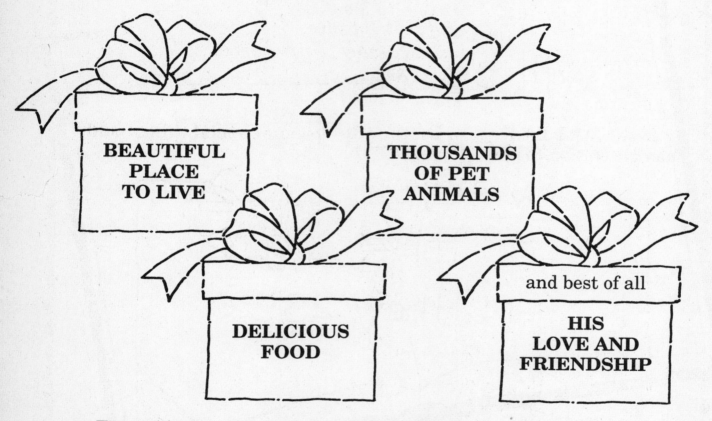

BEAUTIFUL PLACE TO LIVE

THOUSANDS OF PET ANIMALS

DELICIOUS FOOD

and best of all

HIS LOVE AND FRIENDSHIP

Every evening, God would visit Adam and Eve in the beautiful Garden of Eden. God's Word doesn't tell us much about the garden, but we know it had to be the most beautiful garden on earth. It had four sparkling rivers, luscious fruit trees, and lots of gold and precious stones. It also had animals and beautiful flowers that God had created for Adam and Eve to enjoy.

Have you ever wondered what Adam and Eve did all day in the Garden of Eden? God's Word tells us their job was to take care of all of God's animals and plants. What a BIG job! But I'm sure they enjoyed being God's *special* caretakers.

GO

Life in the garden started out perfect. Adam and Eve had perfect bodies, perfect minds, and a perfect friendship with the God who made them and loved them.

God loves **you**, too, and has given you many wonderful gifts to enjoy and take care of.

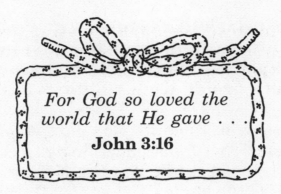

For God so loved the world that He gave . . .

John 3:16

In the gift boxes below, write or draw some special things God has given you to show His love.

The Biggest Blooper

The Fall of Adam and Eve (Genesis 3:1-19)

Templeton and Furlock like riddles. Can you read the Bible story and help them figure out the answers to the riddles below the story? Each answer is a main character in the story. Write your answers beside each riddle.

Do you remember some of the gifts God gave Adam and Eve after He created them? There was something else God gave them when He put them in the beautiful Garden of Eden—a rule. "You can eat of every tree in the garden except one. Do not eat of the tree called 'knowledge of good and evil' or you will die!" Adam and Eve weren't the only ones who heard God's rule that day, for it didn't take long for Satan, God's enemy, to disguise himself as a beautiful animal, called a serpent, to trick Eve into eating that fruit! Then Eve talked Adam into eating some, too. Suddenly they were scared! They knew they had disobeyed God. They hid, but God knew exactly where they were and what they had done. "Because you have disobeyed Me," God said to Adam and Eve, "you must leave the Garden of Eden. You must work hard for your food, pulling weeds and thistles. You will have pain and sickness, and you will die."

1. A most beautiful animal I used to be,
   Until a curse was put on me. Who am I? _____

2. Two perfect people we used to be,
   Until we ate from the forbidden tree. Who are we? _____
   and _____

3. Tricking people is what I do;
   Adam and Eve were the very first two. Who am I? _____

4. I was the saddest one of all
   When Adam and Eve took their great fall. Who am I? _____

ANSWERS: 1. serpent 2. Adam and Eve 3. Satan 4. God

But God still loved Adam and Eve even though they had disobeyed. He wanted to be their friend, so He gave them one more gift . . .

FORGIVENESS

God promised Adam and Eve that someday He would send a Savior down to earth to take the punishment for their sin. Since Adam and Eve sinned, their children were born with a desire to do wrong. You and I were born that way, too. **You** need a Savior just like Adam and Eve did. Who did God send to be our Savior so we could have the gift of forgiveness, too? JESUS! But this gift isn't **your** gift until you take it by asking God to forgive you for the wrong things you've done and to give you everlasting life.

> . . . *Christ [Jesus] died for our sins according to the Scriptures . . . he was buried . . . he was raised [came back to life] on the third day . . . .*
> **1 Corinthians 15:3,4**

Have you received God's gift of forgiveness and everlasting life? If so, color in the gift box above.

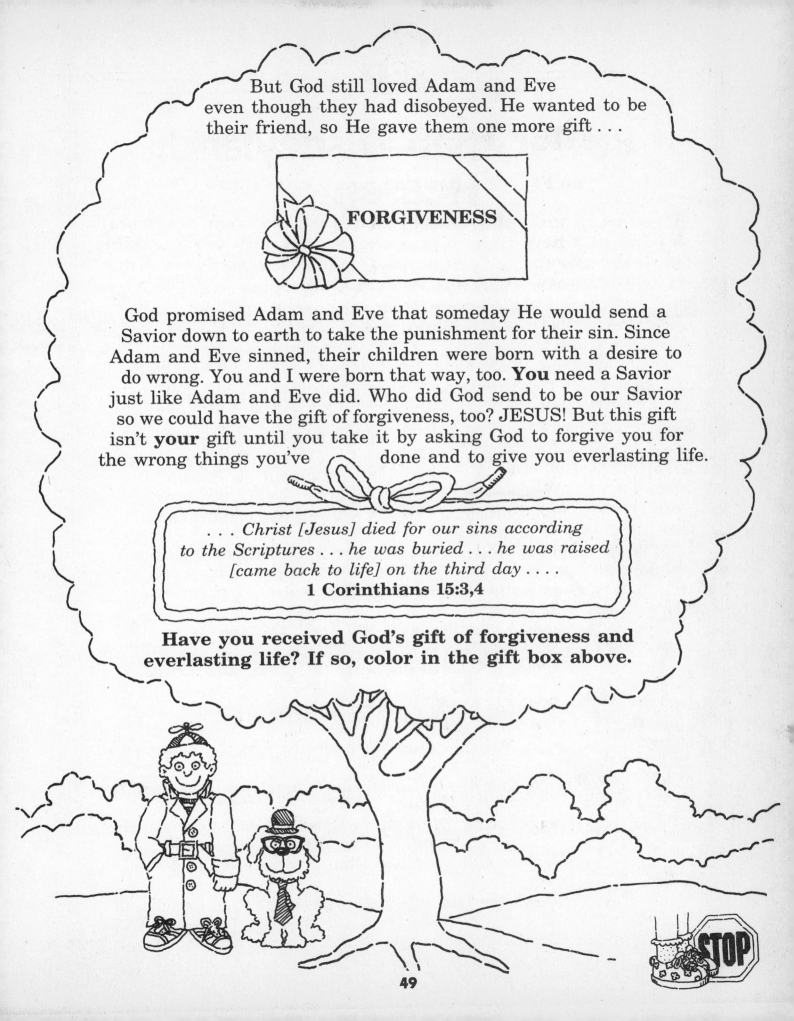

STOP

DAY FIVE

Better than Disneyland: Heaven
(Revelation 21:4,10-22)

For God so loved the world that he gave his one and only Son, that whoever believes in him shall not perish but have eternal life.
John 3:16

Have you ever looked inside an oyster and found a pearl? Pearls are valuable jewels. What is your favorite gem? Is it a diamond? Is it an emerald? The ▭ tells us of a beautiful place which has many precious 💎. Do you know the name of this place? It's heaven, God's home. Heaven has walls of sapphire, topaz, pearls, and emeralds. Heaven also has a ~~~~ of gold, a 🌳 of life with 12 kinds of fruit, thousands of 👥 a crystal-clear river, and much more. All this sounds wonderful, but the best part of all is that Jesus Christ, God's Son, lives in heaven. He is preparing 🏠 for those who will live with Him. Heaven will be better than any vacationland that you've ever visited—yes, even better than Disneyland!

50

Fill in the blanks to discover what will be in heaven. Use the code in the treasure chest.

$$\underset{2}{\quad}\underset{8}{\quad}\underset{6}{\quad}W\underset{5}{\quad}\underset{7}{\quad}\quad M\underset{1}{\quad}\underset{5}{\quad}\underset{7}{\quad}I\underset{6}{\quad}\underset{5}{\quad}\underset{7}{\quad}\quad\underset{1}{\quad}\underset{5}{\quad}\underset{4}{\quad}\underset{3}{\quad}L\underset{7}{\quad}$$

Who will go to God's heaven? Only those who . . .

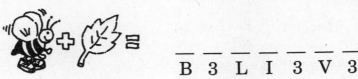

$$\overline{}\ \underset{}{B}\ \underset{}{3}\ \underset{}{L}\ \underset{}{I}\ \underset{}{3}\ \underset{}{V}\ \underset{}{3}$$

Look up John 3:16 to check your answer. Write the verse on the lines below. Color the words, *"whoever believes in Him"* with a crayon or red marker, and *"shall . . . have"* with a crayon or green marker, and *"eternal life"* with a crayon or yellow marker.

_____

_____

_____

God's Map to Heaven: Salvation

For God so loved the world that He gave His one and only Son, that whoever believes in Him shall not perish but have eternal life.

(John 3:16)

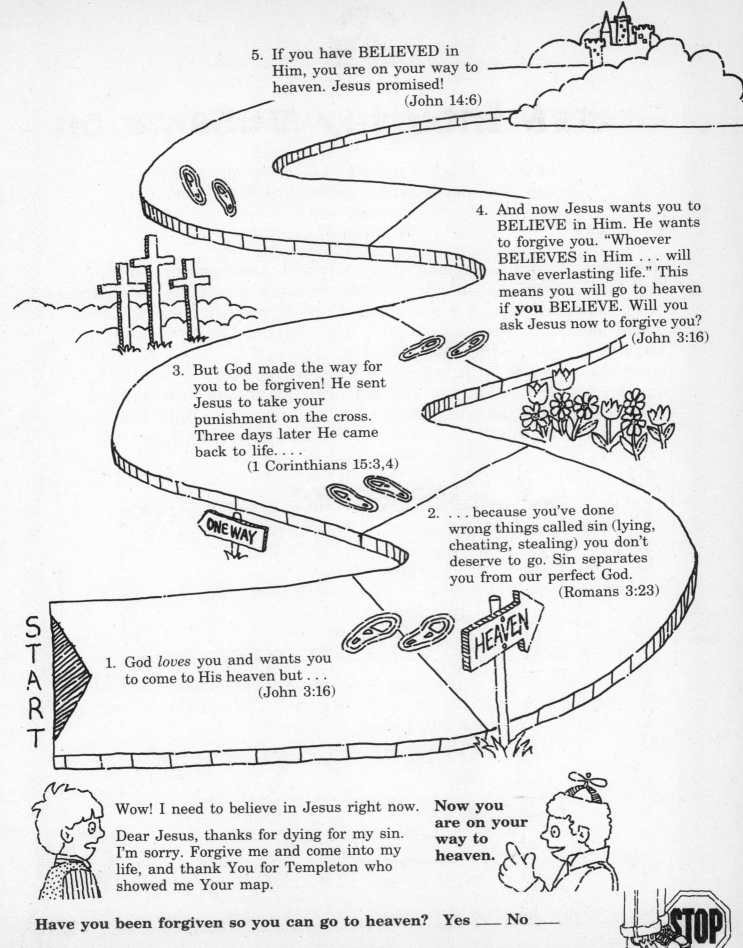

5. If you have BELIEVED in Him, you are on your way to heaven. Jesus promised! (John 14:6)

4. And now Jesus wants you to BELIEVE in Him. He wants to forgive you. "Whoever BELIEVES in Him . . . will have everlasting life." This means you will go to heaven if **you** BELIEVE. Will you ask Jesus now to forgive you? (John 3:16)

3. But God made the way for you to be forgiven! He sent Jesus to take your punishment on the cross. Three days later He came back to life. . . . (1 Corinthians 15:3,4)

ONE WAY

2. . . . because you've done wrong things called sin (lying, cheating, stealing) you don't deserve to go. Sin separates you from our perfect God. (Romans 3:23)

HEAVEN

S T A R T

1. God *loves* you and wants you to come to His heaven but . . . (John 3:16)

Wow! I need to believe in Jesus right now.

Dear Jesus, thanks for dying for my sin. I'm sorry. Forgive me and come into my life, and thank You for Templeton who showed me Your map.

Now you are on your way to heaven.

STOP

Have you been forgiven so you can go to heaven? Yes ___ No ___

53

SUNSHINE JOY
PUG
SLIM
ROCKY
HERBIE

SAM
DOT PORKY
CANDY

Sure Enough: Assurance

*I write these things to you who believe in the name of the
Son of God so that you may know that you have eternal life.*

1 John 5:13
Hebrews 13:5

Do you have a nickname? Renee's friends have nicknamed her
"Sunshine" because she is always smiling and trying to make
others laugh. Renee is a ten-year-old girl who has a serious disease
called leukemia. The doctors have told her that she most likely will
not live to see her fifteenth birthday. How can Renee be so happy
when she is so sick? It is because she believes in Jesus as her Savior
and knows He has forgiven her sins. She knows Jesus is with her
every day and when she dies she will go to heaven. How does she
know this? The Bible clearly says so. She has put her faith in God's
promises. Her two favorite verses are:

*If anyone acknowledges that Jesus is the Son of God,
God lives in him and he in God.*
1 John 4:15
*. . . whoever believes in him [Jesus] shall not perish
but have eternal life.*
John 3:16

Because Renee has believed in Jesus, she is not worried about what
will happen when her life on earth is ended. Instead she is looking
forward to seeing Jesus face-to-face in heaven.

BUCKO
MUFFIE
JACK

TOOTS BIFF
TIFFY

GO

What about you? Are you **sure** that you are going to heaven? The Bible says you can be certain. **Be sure you're sure!**

Read 1 John 5:13. Draw a line from star to star to finish God's promise to you . . .

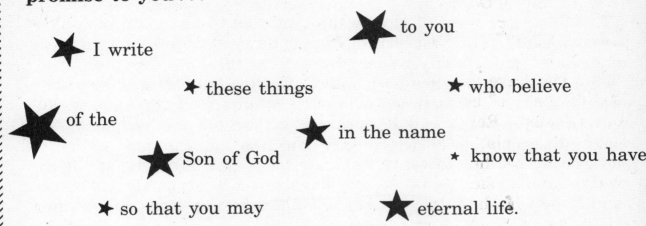

⭐ to you

⭐ I write

⭐ these things   ⭐ who believe

⭐ of the   ⭐ in the name

⭐ Son of God   ⭐ know that you have

⭐ so that you may   ⭐ eternal life.

If you have believed in Jesus, God **promises** you'll go to His heaven someday.

Draw a smiley face in the circle if you are sure that you are on your way to God's home, heaven.

◯

Renee's nickname is Sunshine. Many times a nickname describes the way a person acts or looks.

What would you like your nickname to be? _____

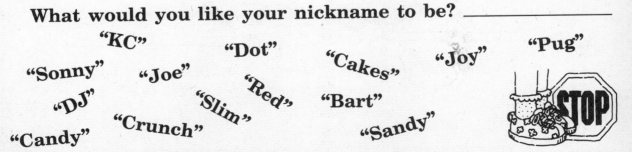

"KC"   "Dot"   "Cakes"   "Joy"   "Pug"

"Sonny"   "Joe"

"DJ"   "Slim"   "Red"   "Bart"

"Candy"   "Crunch"   "Sandy"   STOP

Weekly Verse:
Romans 5:8

Happy Birthday to You: New Life

Birthdays are special! How would you like to have two birthdays each year? Your first birthday is the day you were born into your mom's and dad's family. When you receive the Lord Jesus as your Savior from sin, you are born into God's family. This can be your second birthday. Sometimes when you celebrate the day you were born into your mom's and dad's family you receive gifts. When you're born into God's family, you receive gifts too.

Jesus gives you eternal life. This special verse tells us about it:

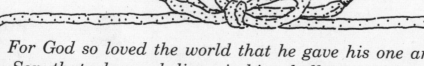

For God so loved the world that he gave his one and only Son, that whoever believes in him shall not perish but have eternal life.
John 3:16

GO

56

Now, let's rewrite it by putting *your* name in the blanks:

For God so loved _____ that He gave His one and only

Son, that if _____ believes in Him, _____ shall

not perish [or be separated from God], but _____ shall

have ETERNAL LIFE.

"Eternal" means that it lasts forever! Even though your body will die, your soul and spirit (the real you) will live with Jesus in heaven forever! Someday God will give you a new body like the Lord Jesus had after He came back to life.

If you have received the Lord Jesus as your Savior, you have this special birthday gift *right now!* How many birthdays do you have?

If you have two birthdays because you've received the Lord Jesus, when is your second one?

_____ _____ _____
     DAY   MONTH   YEAR

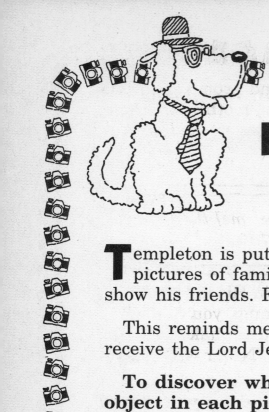

Family Photos: God's Family

(John 1:12)

Templeton is putting together a family album. He's collecting pictures of family members and gluing them in a special book to show his friends. Furlock looks very nice, don't you think?!

This reminds me of one of God's special gifts to you when you receive the Lord Jesus as your Savior.

To discover what it is, write down the first letter of the object in each picture below:

___ ___ ___ ___ ___ ___

What is this gift? A brand new FAMILY! God becomes your heavenly Father, and others who have received the Lord Jesus as their Savior from sin become your new brothers and sisters!

> *Yet to all who received him, to those who believed in his name, he gave the right to become children of God.*
> **John 1:12**

GO

You have a Father in heaven who loves you and promises to take care of you *forever*! Sometimes our earthly father, mother, brothers, or sisters leave us, but God's Word promises,

Though my father and mother forsake [leave] me] the Lord [God] will receive me. **Psalm 27:10**

No matter what you've done, He will let you be in His family. You need to ask Him to forgive you for the wrong things you've done, believe the Lord Jesus died for you, and ask God to make you His child. God has promised as your heavenly Father, "Never will I leave you" (Hebrews 13:5).

Let's put that promise on your fingers. Hold up your hand with the palm of your hand facing you. Say the promise three times, pointing to your fingers as you say the words:

I
WILL
NEVER
LEAVE
YOU

As part of God's family, you have thousands of brothers and sisters all over the world who also have believed in the Lord Jesus.

Can you think of some friends who will be there, too?

Draw their pictures below and make your own "family photo." Don't forget to include yourself!

Meet Your "Stay-Within Friend:" Eternal Security

(Romans 8:38,39)

Why the sad face, Jerry?

My dad promised me he'd help me with my science project tonight. But he, like always, had to go out of town on business. Now what do I do?

That's too bad. I know how it feels.

It always seems that no one is around when you need them!

Jerry, I know someone who is around *any* and *every* time you need Him.

Oh yea? Who is it? Superman?

God is always with you. You are His child since you are a Christian now. He promises "I WILL NEVER LEAVE YOU." He'll be with you when you're at the dentist. He'll be with you on the playground. He'll be with you when you go to sleep at night. HE'S YOUR HEAVENLY FATHER WHO WILL NEVER, EVER LEAVE YOU.

Wow, pretty neat! I have a lot to learn as a new Christian. But, uh, what do I do about my project?

How would it be if I helped you? I love science. Looks like I came along just in time . . .

Great!

Isn't it good to know that *God is always there* to help even when you can't feel or see Him? He has *promised* to be with you forever. And remember: God never 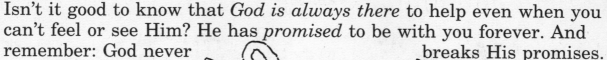 breaks His promises.

Never will I leave you; never will I forsake you.
Hebrews 13:5

Find your way to the finish line to discover God's promise to you. Start at the arrow . . .

Write the promise in the blanks below:

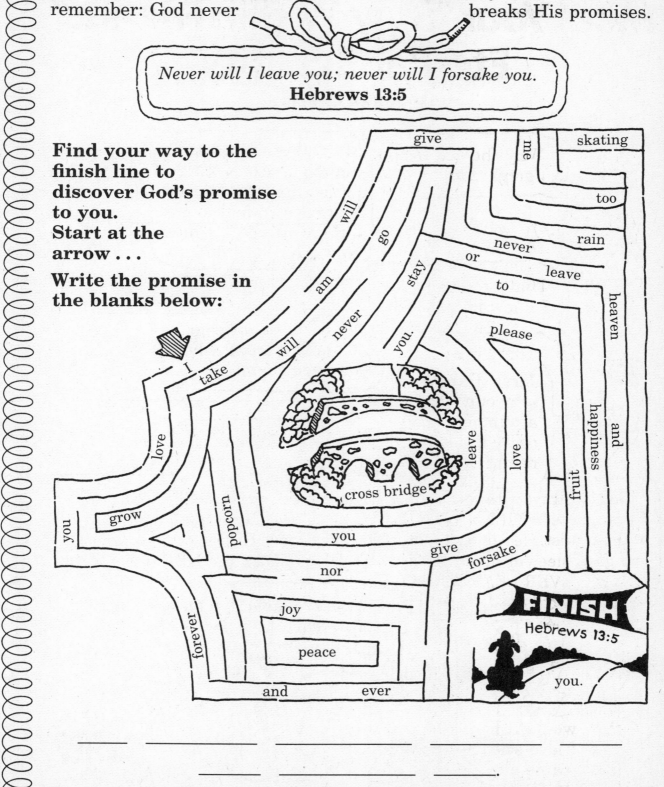

_____

_____

Cross out all the J's and X's to solve the puzzle.

Jesus is with you all the time. He is with you when . . .

. . . you go to the   J D X O C J J T O R X

_____

. . . you are all   A X L J X O N X E X J

_____

. . . you give a report in   J X C L X A S S J

_____

. . . there is a   X H U R R X I C A N E

_____

Hotline to Heaven: Prayer

Even though you probably don't drive, I'm sure you've seen this set of traffic signals before. We can use these signals to help us remember how God answers our prayers. Prayer is talking to God. God always hears your prayers no matter where you are. God can hear you in church, at home, in school, or anywhere. He wants to help you with everything. God cares about your problems, big or small, and God always answers your prayers. Sometimes he says yes ⬤. God wants to bless us and give us everything we need. Sometimes God says no ⬤. A little baby sometimes has to be told no when he wants to play with something dangerous. We need to trust God to tell us no when we ask for something that isn't the best thing for us. Sometimes God says slow down ◯. We may think we are ready for what we ask, but God is wise and will give us what we need at the right time. God knows what will happen in the future, and we can trust Him to make the right choice for us.

For the eyes of the Lord are on the righteous and His ears are attentive to their prayer.
1 Peter 3:12

Answer these questions by writing true or false in the blanks.

1. Prayer is talking to God. _____

2. You can pray anywhere. _____

3. God can only hear you if you pray really loud. _____

4. God sometimes wants us to wait for what we ask. _____

5. God always says yes to our prayers. _____

6. God cares about all of our problems. _____

Answers:
1. True 2. True 3. False
4. True 5. False 6. True

64

The Contest: Prayer Power

. . . he prayed earnestly . . .
James 5:17

We will have a contest and see who answers prayer,
Baal or Jehovah. It is time that we compare.

Ahab and his prophets built an altar made of rocks,
Then placed some wood upon the top and sacrificed an ox.

Not far away Elijah built an altar just the same.
Was he worried? Not at all, he trusted in God's name.

King Ahab and his prophets were the first to make their call:
Dear Baal, please send down fire upon the altar, make it fall.

They cried and cried but finally had to quit.
Their god sent no fire—not even just a bit.

But let us see what happened next for now it's Jehovah's turn.
Elijah called upon the Lord to make the altar burn.

A flash of fire came from heaven—burned all on the altar there.
Everyone saw what God could do when He's called upon in prayer.

(from 1 Kings 18)

I would have liked to have been there to see that contest, wouldn't you? Elijah called on the one true God and He answered. What about you? Do you call on God in prayer? If so, do you mean what you say?

Have you ever heard someone pray at the table like this? "Godsgreat,Gosgood,lettucethankimforrfood . . ." It sounds like a foreign language. Think how God feels when you don't take prayer seriously. The Bible tells us in James 5:17 that Elijah prayed

65

earnestly. That means he prayed with all his heart. Are you earnest when you pray? If so, God will hear and answer your prayers.

God promises that if you ask anything according to His will, He hears you.

(Remember: God doesn't always answer "yes." Sometimes He says "no" or "wait.")

Shade in all the odd-numbered boxes. You will find a special message in the even-numbered boxes.

Write out the words you find in the spaces below the altar:

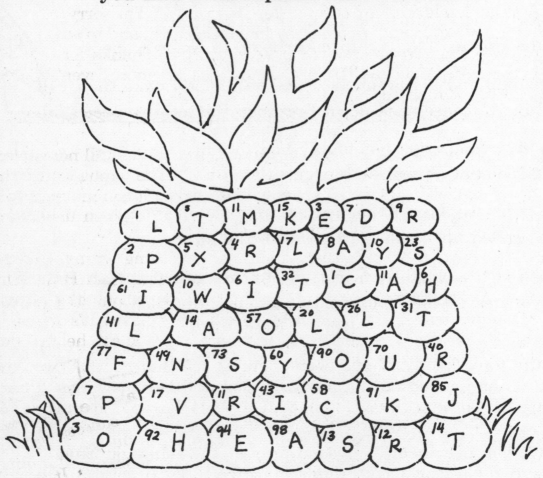

Answer: ___ ___ ___ ___ ___ ___ ___

Pardon Me: Confession

. . . I said, "I will confess my transgressions to the Lord" — and you forgave the guilt of my sin.

Psalm 32:5

Dear God,

Thank You that You hear me all of the time. I know You see me all of the time, too, so You know what just happened. God, I was really scared when I broke that vase. It was just an accident, but Mom looked so mad that I told her my little sister Amy did it. I'm sorry I lied, God. Help me to tell my mom the truth, and to tell Amy I'm sorry for telling a lie about her. Thanks for forgiving me, God. Help me not to lie anymore, even when I'm scared.

After you ask Jesus to come into your heart, you're still not perfect. Sometimes you'll do things that are wrong. The wrong things that we do are called sin. If we let sin stay in our lives, it can make us feel terrible. God doesn't want that to happen, so He's given us a Way of taking care of our sin. It's called *confession*.

Confession is telling God when you do something wrong. God sees everything you do. It's impossible to hide anything from Him. Why do we have to confess our sin if God already knows about it? God wants us to confess our sin so He can be sure that *we* know it's wrong. Confession isn't to help God. Confession is a way God can help us grow closer to Him.

How Do You Confess Sin?
Just tell God what you've done wrong and tell Him you're sorry. Ask Him to help you not to do it again.

When Can We Confess Sin?
It's best to confess right away, as soon as you know you've done something wrong. It doesn't matter what time it is, or where you are. God is always ready to listen.

We don't use a telephone to talk to God, but this phone can give us a special message.

Just follow these directions to fill in the spaces below. The numbers tell you which button to look at. The dots tell you which letter on that button to use. · Tells you to use the first letter. ·· tells you to use the second letter. ··· tells you to use the third letter. Below the first space is a 3···. Find the button with the number 3. Now find the third letter on that button. Did you find the letter I? Put I in the first space and finish the message.

$\overline{3_{···}}\ \overline{2_{···}}\quad\overline{8_{··}}\ \overline{2_{··}}\quad\overline{1_{···}}\ \overline{5_{···}}\ \overline{5_{·}}\ \overline{2_{···}}\ \overline{2_{··}}\ \overline{7_{·}}\ \overline{7_{·}}\quad\overline{5_{···}}\ \overline{7_{···}}\ \overline{6_{···}}$

$\overline{7_{·}}\ \overline{3_{···}}\ \overline{5_{··}}\ \overline{7_{·}}\quad\overline{3_{··}}\ \overline{2_{··}}\quad\overline{3_{···}}\ \overline{7_{·}}$

$\overline{2_{···}}\ \overline{1_{·}}\ \overline{3_{···}}\ \overline{7_{··}}\ \overline{3_{··}}\ \overline{2_{···}}\ \overline{7_{···}}\ \overline{4_{···}}\quad\overline{1_{·}}\ \overline{5_{·}}\ \overline{2_{·}}\quad\overline{8_{··}}\ \overline{3_{···}}\ \overline{4_{···}}\ \overline{4_{···}}$

$\overline{2_{···}}\ \overline{5_{···}}\ \overline{6_{···}}\ \overline{3_{·}}\ \overline{3_{···}}\ \overline{8_{·}}\ \overline{2_{··}}\quad\overline{5_{···}}\ \overline{7_{···}}\ \overline{6_{···}}\quad\overline{7_{·}}\ \overline{3_{···}}\ \overline{5_{··}}\ \overline{7_{·}}$

1 John 1:9

Give It All to God: Consecration

Sometimes, to get things you want, you have to give up other things. If you consecrate yourself to something (the word *consecrate* means to decide to do something and stick with it no matter what), you can do just about anything. That's why after you ask Jesus into your heart, God wants you to consecrate your life to Him. If you consecrate yourself to God, that means you are deciding to do what you know God wants you to do. Think of how much God can do through you if you are consecrated to serving him!

It's easy to say you'll always serve God, but sometimes it's not as easy to do. Templeton had some rough days this week.

What would you do if this happened to you? Would you . . .

Not listen to temptation?

SUNDAY

Let's play ball instead of going to church . . . You aren't chicken are you?

Love others?

TUESDAY

Let's not play with Stinky Sam!

Obey your parents?

FRIDAY

No more cookies until after dinner.

GO

In the Bible, God tells us many things that He wants all Christians to do.

Look these verses up and write what the verse tells you to do on the page in the book. The first one is written in the book for you.

1. Matthew 5:44
2. John 6:43
3. Ephesians 4:29
4. Ephesians 4:32
5. Ephesians 6:1

Now think of what you can do to obey God's commands. Can you be nice to someone who was mean to you, or can you do what your parents tell you without grumbling, even when it's not fun? Write in the book what you can do to obey God's Word. The first one is done for you.

GOD WANTS ALL CHRISTIANS TO DO THIS:

1. Love enemies.

2. _____

3. _____

4. _____

5. _____

SO I CAN OBEY GOD BY DOING THIS:

1. Be nice to Billy, even when he's mean to me.

2. _____

3. _____

4. _____

5. _____

God, please help me to do what I know You want me to do, even when it's hard.

Certificate
of Completion

This Certifies That

_____

has completed Volume One of
Seekers In Sneakers

_____   _____

Parent   **Date**

"Love the Lord your God with all your heart and with all
your soul and with all your mind and
with all your strength"
(Mark 12:30)

Genesis 1:31a

"God saw all that He had made and it was very good."

Romans 5:8

"But God demonstrates his own love for us in this: While we were still sinners, Christ died for us."

Isaiah 44:6b

"...I am the first and I am the last; apart from me there is no God."

Hebrews 13:5b

"...God has said, 'Never will I leave you; never will I forsake you.'"